I Just Wan

Fredricka Thelwell

SURPLUS
LIBRARY OF
CONGRESS
DUPLICATE

VANTAGE PRESS
New York

FIRST EDITION

All rights reserved, including the right of
reproduction in whole or in part in any form.

Copyright © 1997 by Fredricka Thelwell

Published by Vantage Press, Inc.
516 West 34th Street, New York, New York 10001

Manufactured in the United States of America
ISBN: 0-533-11913-8

Library of Congress Catalog Card No.: 96-90128

0 9 8 7 6 5 4 3 2

My daughter, Elizabeth Thelwell, was born on March 23, 1994. When traveling around by train, bus, or car, I got so much help from people who would open doors for me, help with folding or lifting the stroller, or even give up their seat on a train or bus. This wonderful help inspired me to write "I Just Want to Say Thank You." The help has always been appreciated, whether by me or anyone who receives a helping hand. Those people who help are appreciated each and every day and so I just want to give something back by saying "Thank you."

Contents

Introduction

In this world of conservative,
Violence, hardship, and pain,
"We see it each day."

"There is another side of this world,"
The side that is kind, generous,
Warm hearted, loving,
Reaching out for each other,
Helping out—no matter how hard
It may be.

There are thousands of different kinds
Of jobs in this world.
It's admirable, people respecting people,
Whether communicating with the public
Or just having to be around each other,
Day by day.

"It brings tears to your eyes,
Joy to your heart. Can people be so kind,
So polite?"
Talking to you on the phone is a pleasure,
Your going that extra mile to help.
Answering many questions,
Over and over, again and again,
With smiles and politeness, time after time.

"It's not about the pay."
Love and respect taught in the home,
Demonstrated from the heart.

Passion and reflection,
From all directions.
There is kindness in the air,
Blowing all over everywhere.

We don't have to agree with
Each other's opinion,
But show each other love.
Yes, there is hate,
But there's certainly more and more
Love that binds us, day after day.

It's good to know people care for each other,
Customers, getting more deals.
We see more products having more and more inside.
It would be great to see every product with a percentage.
It's good to know manufacturers and entrepreneurs are
Thinking about the customers,
Giving more of a percentage, more value for our money.

You Show that Love Is Never Too Much to Give

You show that love
Is never too much to give.
You show the meaning
Of love in every way.
By generosity,
Giving and sharing your love,
You can see that you are abundantly blessed.

Even when you seem tired,
When it comes to giving
And sharing your love,
You are never tired.

Love, love, love.
Love, love, love.
You give it all the time;
It's like you are wired;
May you be loved always
And be blessed,
All the rest of your life.
Thank you.

For Society They Always Care

Whether it's a disaster
Or doing something good,
They are always there;
For society they always care.

Risking their lives,
Forgetting all about themselves,
Leaving their families,
Anything they were
Doing behind.

When disasters strike,
It's rush, rush, rush,
Rushing like crazy
To give a helping hand.

They think fast
To help me and you,
Leaving behind things
They were doing,
Sometimes eating,
Taking a nap,
Refreshment,
Shower, anything.

Rushing to help,
Rushing to help.
To you, we say many thanks.
May many blessings pour
Upon you and your family,
From our heart to yours.
Thank you.

From My Heart I Say Thanks

You didn't have to swear;
You said "I will."
You went out of your way,
But you helped me.

You looked straight in my eyes.
From your mouth
You said, in a positive voice,
"Don't worry,
I am going to help you,"
You said from your heart.

I lift my glass to you.
I can see the good today
That came out of what
You did for me yesterday.

You are a picture of harmony.
From my heart I say thanks
You are always remembered.
May happiness be with you
And yours always,
Forever
Thank you.

Thank You for Being So Special

I just want to say,
"Thank you for being so special."
When it comes to love,
Honesty,
Respect,
Motivation.
You've got it all in place.

Thank you not only
For loving me,
But also for respecting
My feelings.
For respecting me
As a human being.
Thank you.

Risking Their Lives

Risking their lives
To go in search;
To go under,
To go up,
To go around,
To go in and out.

Sometimes minutes,
Hours, days, nights.
Some lose their lives,
Some lives change for good.

Life is all about love,
People helping people,
Being there for one another.
May happiness be with you
And yours always.
Thank you.

I Love Your Work of Art

You create magnificent
Works of art.
I respect your work;
I admire your art.

Art in every form,
Paint, shape or ways.
Looking in I disappear in it,
Sometimes it seems,
So real.

Great art, newly art;
Art of the century,
Small art, big art.
I love your work of art.

Path of Peacefulness

I am so happy you helped
To make peace.
You guard us along
That path of peacefulness.

You fill that gap,
With floating rivers of love.
You explain to us,
Why we should love one another.

You insist upon harmony,
Peace and love.
You said, "Love each other;
Time is too short,
For your bloodstream to be
Flowing with hate.

"You don't have to
Argue with each other;
Peace is so much better."
Thanks for your encouragement.
I feel at peace with myself.
Thank you.

Great Friend

Your humor goes with
Your gratitude;
Your appearance from inside
And outside is generous.
You are honest, kind
And humorous;

You share your ideas.
You listen to mine.
You are not selfish;
I love that about you.

You are so fabulous.
For being there I would like
To say "Thank you!"
With great joy,
I show my gratitude.
I love being your friend.
Thank you.

You Believe in Me

Thank you, so much, for believing in me.
Thank you, so much, for trusting me.
Thank you, for being there for me.
Thank you, for taking care of me.
Thank you, for giving me good directions,
In every way so nicely.
Thanks for your good reaction.
Thank you! For your love and all the above.

Great Memory

As I look at your picture,
I see love.
As I look at your picture,
Oh! what great memory.
As I look at your picture,
I have to smile.
As I look at your picture,
I start thinking,
Isn't life wonderful?

Thanks, Mother

Thanks, Mother, for growing us
With your love.
Thanks, Mother, for growing us
With kindness;
Thank you for making it
Possible for us,
To be ourselves and what we are.
You've revived us with love.
You guided us through thick,
through thin.
Thanks for teaching us
Such important things.

Thank You for Waiting

You did not give up on me.
I trusted you;
But deep in my mind
I wondered if you would
Wait for me.

The truth is I was not sure.
When I saw you wait so long,
I realized I was so wrong.
I did not know you'd wait
But you did wait, and wait.

With tears in my eyes
I want to say,
"Thank you for waiting.
I will always love you."

Woman of Great Courage

You are a woman of great courage;
I admire you.
You are a woman with lots of love;
I respect you.
You are fun;
You are of great joy.

"You are like a flower
That is always blooming!"
Kindness runs through your veins,
Like a river.

Bending over, you whisper
In my ears, "I love you."
The touch of your hands
Is like gold.
You are very, very special.

You are a beauty,
Right from your heart;
Like an angel, you shine.

Like a little duckling,
Floating on top of the water,
You are watchable.

Uprise, downfall
You are always there,
Giving your family
Tender loving care.

I just want to say,
"You'll always be loved
From the heart."
We say thank you.

Gentleman

Gentleman,
Did you know that
You are very well admired!
You are very well respected!

The way you take care
Of your child—
With tears in my eyes,
I admire you.
People you don't know
Admire you.

Taking care of your child
In such a caring,
Respectable,
Loving way:
It's such a blessing.

You love your child;
You respect your child;
You care for your child.
You are a good man,
You are a great dad,
I am sure you will hear
Thank you over and over again
Now and in years to come.

Oh, How Wonderful

Feel the wind blowing in your face,
Blowing through your clothes,
When sitting anywhere,
Watching the moonlight glow.

Everything came to a stop,
All I was thinking and saying
"What a wonderful world."
No time to think negative,
"Just for the beauty of the world."
"Oh, how marvelous."

Sea and all that's in it,
Mountains short and tall.
Flower, oh, how beautiful,
Baby, what a blessing.

Human body function so magnificent,
The sky's colorful birds,
Beautiful clouds,
The falling rain.
It's a beautiful world.
"Oh, how wonderful."

Helping Hand

"There goes another
Helping hand today!"
Every day there are
Helping hands,
Helping other people.

There is a lot of love
In this world, today.
We can overcome with it
Whatever goes bad.

Loving each other,
Helping other people.
It's so great;
It's of joy;
It's a pleasure;
It's love—
People helping people.

May you have peace
And happiness,
May the same love
And interest you
Have for others
Be given to you.

Thank you for your
Kindness;
Thanks for helping.

You Are Funny

"Yes, yes, yes!"
You are funny!
Are you funny?
Yes, you are!
Funny, funny, funny.

When you talk
It's always funny.
Laughter, laughter,
Tears running from my eyes,
Mixed with laughter.

If I am sad for a moment,
Listening to your jokes
Keeps me blooming.

Laughter is good
For the mind.
"Laughter is fun."
If it's a funny comedy show
Or someone who's funny,
I enjoy the fun;
Thank you.

You Will Always Be Remembered

You show your love,
Care, help, by giving;
No matter how big or small,
You contribute to many affairs.

You show so much love
For yourself and others;
You are the true meaning
Of what love means.

It's not the big or
The small things you do;
It's just doing something;
Loving, caring, sharing
Are beautiful deeds.

Your beauty inside
Always counts.
Helping from the heart
Is blessing.
You have helped
And touched so many people.

You have been appreciated
By so many.
May you always be blessed,
You will always be remembered.
Thank you.

Advertised

"It's been advertised all over!"
But hardly been seen in any store
Or on any shelf.
Seeing the commercials all the time,
Not seeing your product is not a good sign.

Yes, I bought it before.
Yes, manufacturer, please have it in the store.
It's great, but I see it no more.

I saw it advertised, so many times.
Went in search, but could not find.
Customers are getting upset;
Put out more product, we need to get;
Please put out a lot, more of your best.
Thank you.

Someone Cares

You didn't have to smile;
You didn't have to say anything,
But you did.

You say kind words each day;
"How are you?
Thank you!
Be careful!
Have a nice day!
Have a good weekend!
Watch your steps now!"

You make me feel a lot better
By saying those magic words.
In this world today,
It's nice to know someone cares.

From the Heart

Thank you very much,
For helping me.
When I see the good
That came out of what
You did for me,
I sit and cry.

You didn't have to,
But you did.
You went out of your way.
It was hard,
But you did not tell me "no."

You looked straight in my eyes,
Took my hand.
From your heart,
You said in a soft voice,
"I am going to do my best
To help you."
How fascinating, genuine
You are.
Thank you.

Success in the End

I always wanted to do that,
When I was much younger.
You said, "Why not go for it now?"
I gave out a loud ah, ah, ah
Backed up by some good laughter.

It sounded so funny to me,
But you were silent,
Staring into my eyes,
You had no smile,
You were not sharing my laughter.

"Why not think about it," you said.
"Give it a try, you are not too
Old to dream and achieve.
It's reality, don't be deceived.

"Make a start, make a try.
I am one hundred percent
Beside you."
I did try. I am reaping
Success in the end.
Today I want to say,
Thank you.

Thanks for Your Joy

Thank you for making me laugh.
After your birth, I cried for joy!
You bring so much joy
And meaning to my life.
You are indeed amazing.
You make me think of life
In a different way.

Oh, my baby! You are the
Pride and joy of my life.
You are more precious than gold.
I'll watch you like a mother bird.
You are indescribable.
Thanks for your joy.
I am so proud of you.
I love you always.

Toiling Along

Their jobs are outside
In the open world.
Rain or shine they toil along,
They work in different ways,
Day after day,
Sometimes for hours with overtime.
Good, hard, tiresome all combine.
Doing their job with love
And pride,
Thank you!
Yours was a job well done.

You Are a Man of Courage

You are a man of courage;
You are a man of dignity;
You are a man of love;
You are amazing;
You are fun.

Thanks for caring;
Thanks for sharing;
Thanks for your love
And your respect.

Because of your respect,
I cherish you.
Your understanding,
Your intelligence,
Mean so much to me.

For your effort, love
And affection,
I applaud you.
Thanks for your assistance,
Your existence,
For your very good care,
You will always be loved.
THANK YOU.

Make a Start You Just Cannot Tell

Believing in myself
Saying, "I am going to try that tomorrow."
Tomorrow comes, it's next week.
Next week, it's next month.
Next month, it's the middle of the year,
The middle of the year, it's new year's resolution.

"It's a cycle," going around year after year.
But lo and behold, today it's a start.
Two weeks later it's a challenge.
A month later it's good.
In the middle of the year, it's better;
At the end of the year, it's best.

Thinking to myself now,
Why didn't I make a start four years ago?
Maybe it would have been so much better.

Make a start in whatever you want.
You just cannot tell what may happen!
Hey! "Well, go ahead," make a start.
"You just cannot tell."
"If you can't!" by yourself,
Ask somebody for some help.

Grandpa Grandpa

Grandpa, Grandpa
I love you so much,
You read stories,
You tell stories of long ago;
Some make tears come to my eyes.
Thanks, Grandpa!
I've learned a lot from your stories.

Thank you, Grandpa,
For teaching me so many things:
Life, society, memories,
My culture, great knowledge,
And just little things, Grandpa!
Simple things.

Thanks, Grandpa!
For answering all my questions!
Most of all your love.
Thanks for letting me know
You are there for me.
Thank you, Grandpa.
I love you.

My Lovely Pet

You are my lovely pet,
You are my very good friend.
You look on my face,
To show your love.
You are funny!

We have fun playing together.
You are like a tree,
Green and beautiful.
You are always beside me.
You are so loyal.

You are compassionate,
You are inspiring,
You are a part of my family,
And I love you,
Reliable,
Affectionate,
Dedicated friend.

You are my pet;
I love you.
Thanks for being there.

Shining Like a Star

Love yourself;
Give respect;
Show mercy;
Show love;
Don't give up;
Try to make up.

Make peace;
Show peace;
Encourage peace;
Live what is good.

Give back;
Pay back;
Try not to fall
Into any trap.

Take a break;
Play it safe.
Do it right;
Keep it bright.

You are so bold,
Go for that goal.
Don't drink and drive,
You must realize!

If you fall,
Stand up tall.
Be proud of who you are;
Shine, shine, like a star.

Let nothing stop
In your way!
You can make it;
You can do it;
You will make it!
I say, I say, I say,
Yes, yes, yes.

Friends We Are Forever

My child, my child, my child.
You bring tears
Of joy to my eyes.

Thank you, my child
For your love;
Thank you, my child
For all those hugs.

Thank you, my child;
You make me proud.
Thank you, my child;
You make me realize
True love is always around,
Never seems to die.

Friends we are forever.
Upon each other
We can rely.
With all my love,
I say to you,
Thank you,
My child, my child, my child.

You Are a Woman

You are a woman;
You are a lady.
I respect you;
I honor you.

I love you
For what you are.
You are like
A precious stone,
Words cannot describe.

You are a woman;
You are a lady.
Your charming
And smiling face
Is like an "angel's
Glorifying grace."
May you be blessed always.
Thank you, Lady.

Words of Comfort

Thank you for your kind
Words of comfort.
I failed once;
I failed again.
You said, "Try again!"
I told myself,
I will never make it,
You told me,
"You can make it,"
I was thinking negatively;
You said think positively.

I said I fail;
You said you pass.
I said, "I'll never
Reach the top."
You said, "You can make it
To the top,
And if you fall
Just start climbing again."

You said, "Try and try
Again and again;
Don't you ever give up."
Thank you;
You give me hope.

Someone Who Cares

I finally got through
To someone who cares;
I finally got through
To someone
Who speaks to me nicely;
I finally got through
To someone with no
Dirty attitude.

Someone to talk to me
With love in the heart,
Someone to talk
To me with care;
I got someone
To talk to me
In a nice and mannerly way.
I feel like someone;
Thank you. I appreciate you.

A Life of Joy

Pain, pain,
Unbearable pain!
Twist of face,
Tightened fist;
Groaning sound
From my mouth.

Feel like gripping
Someone, anyone—
Doctor, nurse, husband
Boyfriend, relative, friend,
Gripping and never
Letting go.

Holding on for dear life,
While a dear little life
Is wanting to meet the world;
Push, push, push;
Out, out, out.
A life!
A cry, of joy!

I swear, my little angel,
I'll take good care of you;
I will never hurt you;
I am very thankful
To have you come into my life.

My Child, My Baby

"Before you were born,
I loved you,"
Beautiful, innocent, adorable.

I promise
I'll never stop
Loving you.

My child, my baby
So precious
"Seeing you grow
is so wonderful!"
You make me laugh;
You bring me joy and happiness.
For you, I'll do my best;
I promise.

Sister

My sister!
Thank you,
For being there.
For caring,
For sharing.

"Sis," your inspiration
Is so strong,
Thanks for being
There all along.
"Sis," I want you to know
You are very precious.

We promised each other to
Be there for each other.
I appreciate you
For being there,
When I need you most.

Loving one another
Is the best gift of all.
In my heart I say
A little prayer.
Everything is going
To be all right, Sis.
Thanks, I love you.

You Are Admired

"You are the voice of the people."
You are the voice of love,
Talking, talking, talking.

When you talk, people listen;
You are an inspiration.
You will always be remembered for
That voice of yours,
Speaking up, speaking out.

Just like it is,
You say it great,
Loud and clear,
You are admired
By so many.
Thank you.

I Will Remember You Always

Thank you, Teacher,
For helping me reach my goal,
For great encouragement.
For taking time out with me,
Through my problem.

For letting me know
I can reach the top,
For letting me know that
Doing the right thing
Is so much better than
Doing the bad.

Dear Teacher,
I will remember you always,
Even when I grow old,
Because there will always
Be a special place
In my heart for you.

Thanks, Teacher; I love you, Teacher,
You are the best, and so am I
Because of you.
Again thank you.

Thanks for the Push

I try again,
But one more time—
Disappointment;
One more time
Feel like crying,
Feel like running,
Feel like dying,
Feel like stop trying.

"Don't you give up!"
"You can."
Let me tell you a story!
Try again.
Go for it;
No need to feel like dying.

Again and again
I got words of encouragement;
I picked myself up,
Brushed myself off.
There I go again;
I am going to get it this time.
I swear.
Thanks for the push.

Learning from Your Programs

I've learned a lot
From your programs;
Each day you teach the world
Something different.

Whether it's about our children,
Health, entertainment.
I've learned things I need to know
Or simply never knew,
Different kinds of safety.

You give information,
Information, information.
Thanks for continuing to be a
Reliable station.

May you continue to be
The people's most watched station;
In every way, there is always
Something to learn each day.

Putting All into Your Making

You put your all into
Your making;
And whatever else,
You do best.
Beautiful, delicious, catering.

You always make "the best
Meal there is."
Anything you make
Is just great,
Whether you cook at home or not.

You cook to feed the
Hungry and the poor,
As your career,
Or just to enjoy
Making and giving
People the staff of life.

I give you four stars
For what you do best;
We say thanks;
It was good;
It was great;
It was wonderful.

Sing Me Another Song

Please, please
Sing me another song.
Each song you sing
My heart keeps melting.

Inspiring words;
Great, beautiful tune.
You sing with true meaning;
It gives great joy listening
To your encouraging words.

Each time you sing,
It's with more pride,
More joy.
I cannot wait for you
To sing another song.

Each time you give me,
Something to consider;
Thank you for those beautiful words,
One after the other.

Remarkable, magnificent
Lovable.
You have been loved by so many,
Sing another one soon.
We thank you;
We love you.

Great Hero

You are a great soldier;
With brilliance you deliver.
Triumphantly, you are a hero.
You are humble, you are magnifying.
You do your job
With pride and hope;
Your braveness is courage;
Your courage is power;
Your pride is high;
Your willingness is moving.
Brilliant, brave, humble,
You are admired.
You are a great hero;
You are a soldier;
You are love.
Thank you.

Thank You Teacher

You are a teacher
Who has made such a difference
In so many lives.
"You sure make one in mine!"

By giving so much of your time,
Teaching in many languages and signs.
"You don't care a damn about the dime!"
You may not know it,
But your name is so very frequently called.

They talk about your patience, kindness
And caring ways.
Your smile, your love
For what you do best.
They live in many different places;
They speak about you in many
Different ways.

You deserve a standing ovation;
You are a wonderful teacher;
You are loved by so many.
Thank you teacher.

Voice of Love

Your voice is so awesome.
You sing with words of meaning;
You sing like a nightingale;
Your music is like a breath of fresh air.

Singing sensation, singing with such
Meaning and imagination.
Pure, truthful, great, sizzling.
You sing with such pride and joy.
May your voice be strong.
Your music is worth the listening.

Words of Encouragement

Don't you dare give
Up hope now;
Anything is possible,
If you work hard
For what you believe in.

Make a start!
Go for what you want.
Believe in what you do;
Believe in yourself.

Put your mind
To what you do;
Never stop trying;
You can be successful
In what you do!

Don't give up;
Keep your hopes up
High, high, high;
You can reach your goal.
Thank you
For words of encouragement.

Movement

Movement, movement, movement!
Shaking, dancing, tapping, singing,
Putting their whole heart,
Mind, and body—
Acting, dancing, reciting.
Putting everything into
What they do best!

Act of love, memory, courage,
Doing what they do best,
With great joy and pleasure.
Great amazement, great performance.
Movement, movement, movement.
Year after year, I enjoy.
Thank you.

The Letter

You wrote me a letter
And it touched my heart
As I read so many lovely
And meaningful words that are
So touching;
Each time I gaped.
I smiled, I cried.

So much inspiration,
I was deeply moved,
I really need to read
Something like this.

The words are so
Magnificent;
So significant!
Your letter came right
In time
To touch my wearing mind.
Thank you.

I Give You Four Stars

I give you four stars
For walking away;
People admire you,
For walking away from
That fight.

You didn't have to,
But you did;
That's all that matters.

You are a genius;
People respect you
So much that others
Follow in your footsteps.
Others pray for you.

You show love,
Hope, inspiration.
Violence does not pay.
It's very costly;
It can take something
From you, even your life.

Life is not worth that.
In the end you'll find out
Just walking away, pays.
Thank you.

My Brother

My Dear Brother;
You said you'll be my friend,
You will be there for me, to the end.
You said you'll protect me
Even take care of me.
You are always happy for me;
You are always there for me;
You teach me things I did not know.
You love your sister; "Yes!" It shows.
We have our arguments;
We disagree with each other sometimes,
But then again there is sufficient love,
To move any mountain.
I love you, "Brother."
Thank you.

My Favorite Restaurant

The most delicious,
Go with such great attitudes.
Smiles and politeness
Go with your good taste
And all your delightness,
Smiling people, clean environment,
Good enjoyment, comfortable,
Reliable, clean, affordable,
Tasty, enjoyable.
I always look forward to
My favorite restaurant.
Thank you.

The Game I Love

Sometimes we win;
Sometimes we lose;
Sometimes up;
Sometimes down;
Win or lose, I applaud you.
You play earnestly;
You play honestly.

A real game is my enjoyment;
My pleasure.
Now and always.
The "Game I love!"

Legend

In every way you
Are a legend.
A legend indeed you are,
Fearless,
Tireless,
Ambitious.

Wonderful,
Delightful,
Magnificent,
Creative.

In truth
You are loved;
"How lovely you are!"
May you and yours be
Blessed forever.
You have worked hard,
Very hard.
Thank you, legend.